WITHDRAWN

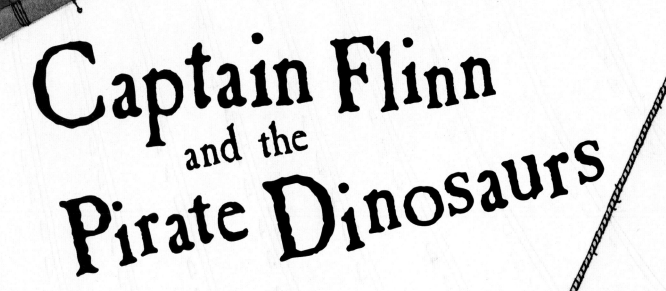

Captain Flinn
and the
Pirate Dinosaurs

Written by
Giles Andreae

Illustrated by
Russell Ayto

Margaret K. McElderry Books
NEW YORK LONDON TORONTO SYDNEY

Margaret K. McElderry Books
An imprint of Simon & Schuster Children's Publishing Division
1230 Avenue of the Americas, New York, New York 10020
Text copyright © 2005 by Giles Andreae
Illustrations copyright © 2005 by Russell Ayto
First published in Great Britain in 2005 by Puffin,
Penguin Books Ltd.
First U.S. edition, 2005

The text for this book is set in Jacoby Light.
The illustrations for this book are rendered in watercolor and ink.
Manufactured in China
6 8 10 9 7 5
CIP data for this book is available from the Library of Congress.
ISBN 1-4169-0713-0 (ISBN-13: 978-1-4169-0713-8)
0615 PUK

For Flinn—G. A.
For my brother—R. A.

This is Flinn.
He is wearing his pirate T-shirt and
coloring in a picture he has drawn of a dinosaur.
Flinn LOVES dinosaurs.

One day at school, Flinn was coloring in a new
dinosaur picture when he realized he didn't have
quite enough markers.

"Why don't you have a look in the supply closet, Flinn?"
said Miss Pie, his teacher. "I think there are
more colors at the back."

So Flinn opened the door

  and stepped

     into

        the

           closet.

There were lots of paints and rolls of paper and pots of glue, but Flinn couldn't see any markers.

As he searched, he heard a noise.

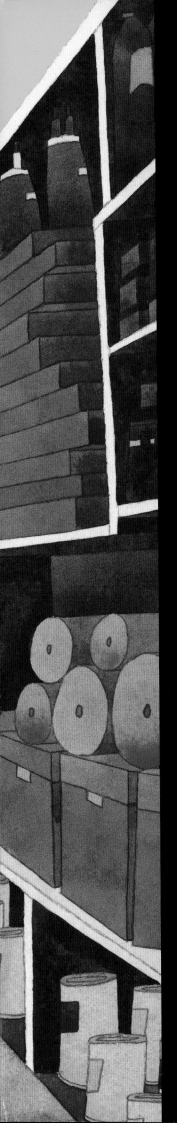

"Boo-hoo!
Boo-hoo-hoo!
Boo-hoo!"

And then,

"Sniffle,
snuffle,
sniffle."

Right at the back of the closet,
under an old curtain, was something
shaking and shuddering.

Flinn crept closer and closer. When he
lifted up the curtain . . .

he couldn't believe his eyes!

It was a real live
PIRATE CAPTAIN!

"Hello," said Flinn. "What's the matter?"

The pirate, whose name was Captain Stubble, sniffed and looked at Flinn.

"My ship! They've stolen my ship!" he sobbed. "One minute I was fast asleep and the next I was in the water watching my precious ship, the *Acorn*, sail away."

"But who has stolen it?" asked Flinn.

"I don't know," said Captain Stubble, "but as I watched, I heard a . . .

ROAR!

. . . and then a strange kind of song.

It went: 'Yo ho ho!
Yo ho ho!

Somethingy,
something

Go! Go! Go!'"

"Hmmm, very strange," said Flinn. "How will you get your ship back?"

"I don't know," blustered Captain Stubble. "I can't do it on my own!"

"I could help," said Flinn bravely.

"And so will we!" It was Flinn's friends, Pearl, Tom, and Violet.

"We love adventures!" they said.

And just at
that moment,
the back
of the closet
fell away and they
all tumbled out . . . .

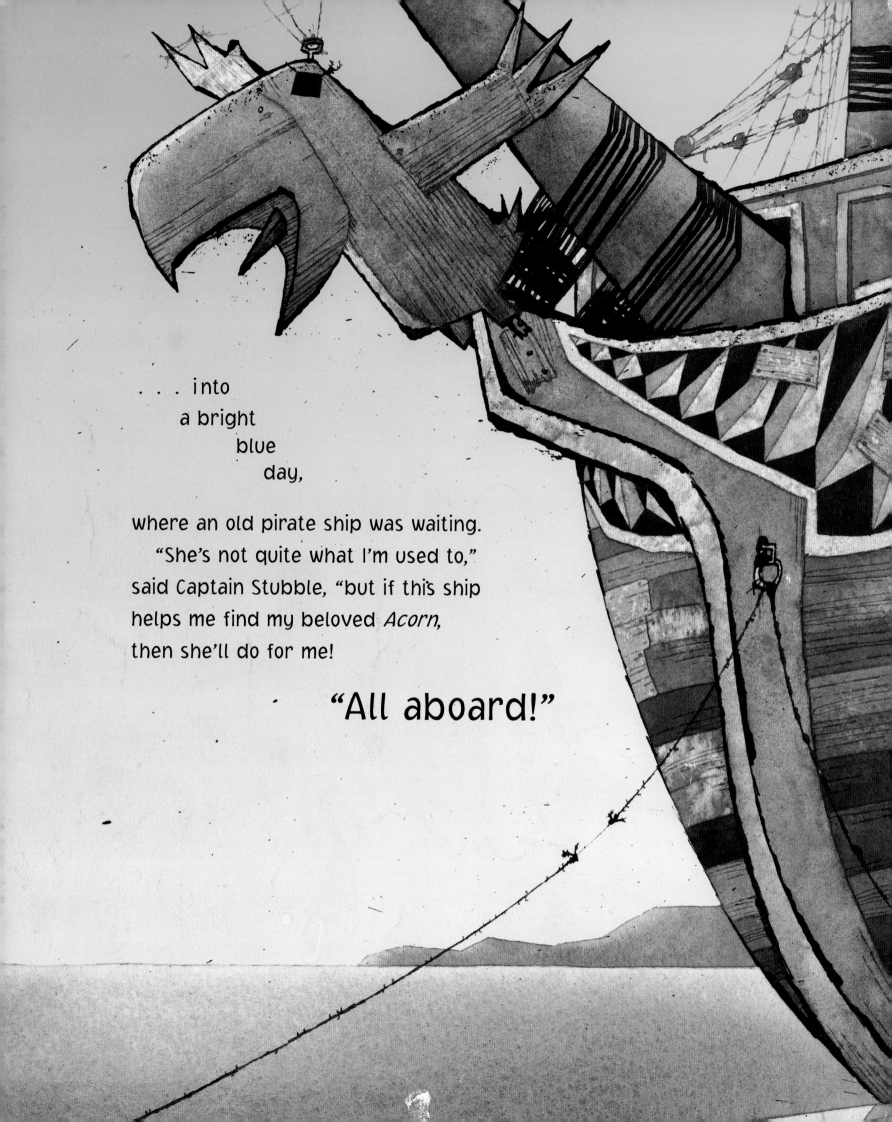

. . . into
a bright
blue
day,

where an old pirate ship was waiting.
"She's not quite what I'm used to,"
said Captain Stubble, "but if this ship
helps me find my beloved *Acorn*,
then she'll do for me!

"All aboard!"

"Right, me hearties," said Captain Stubble. "If you're going to be pirates, you'll need to look like pirates."

Flinn brandished a gleaming silver sword.

"And since you seem to be so brave, Flinn," Captain Stubble said, "you can be captain of this ship. I'd much rather be the cook."

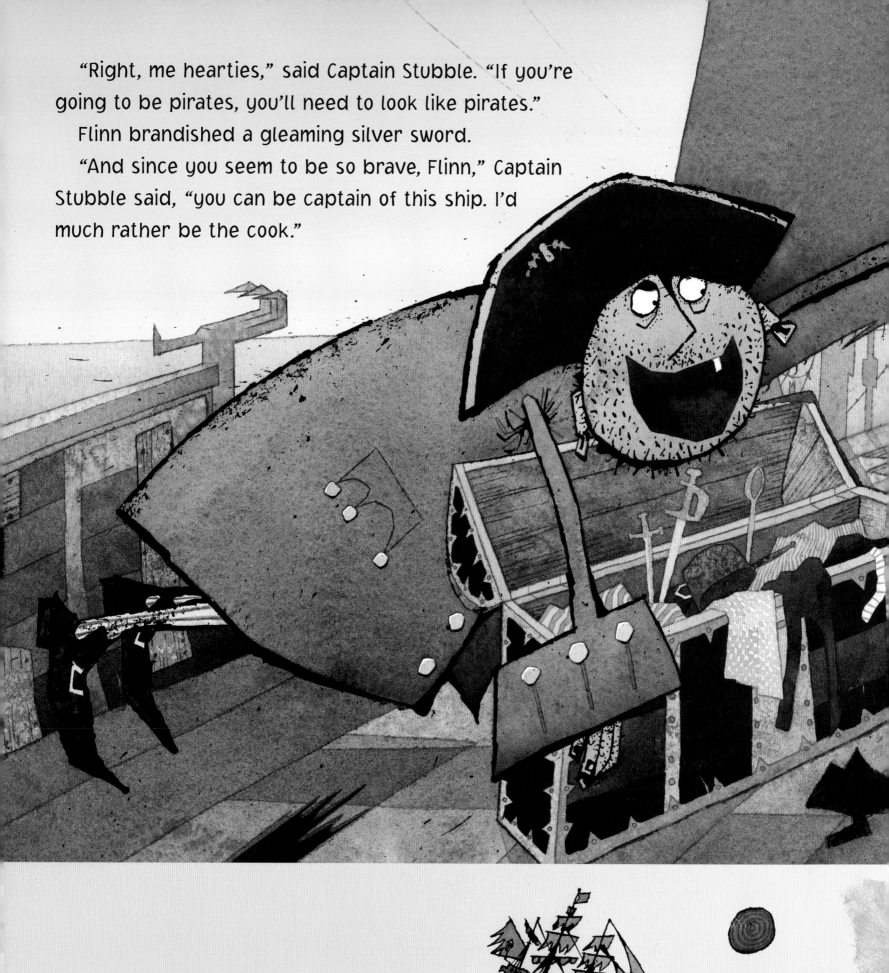

So Captain Flinn took over, and they sailed . . .

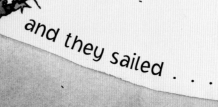

and sailed . . . .

in search of the Acorn.

The pirates were about to give up hope, when Pirate Violet shouted from the crow's nest,
"SHIP AHOY!"

Stubble grabbed his telescope. "That's m
precious *Acorn*!" he cried.
"LET'S BOARD IT!" cried Captain Flinn.
"And reclaim your ship from those pirate
bad guys! ALL HANDS ON DECK!"

They sailed faster and faster and got closer and closer.

When they were nearly alongside the ship, Captain Flinn put the telescope to his eye. His face went white.

"They're not just ordinary pirates," he stammered. "They're . . .

". . . PIRATE DINOSAURS!"

And that is exactly what they were.

There was a pirate diplodocus . . .

a pirate stegosaurus . . .

a pirate triceratops . . .

and a pirate pterodactyl!

And, right at the helm of the ship, steering its course with his claws on the wheel, was a

GREAT . . . BIG . . . PIRATE . . .

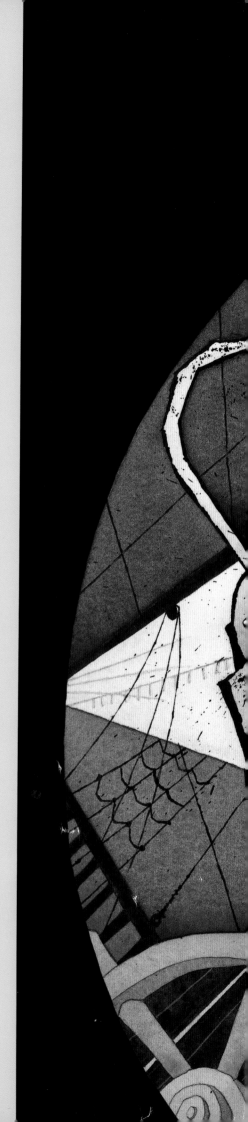

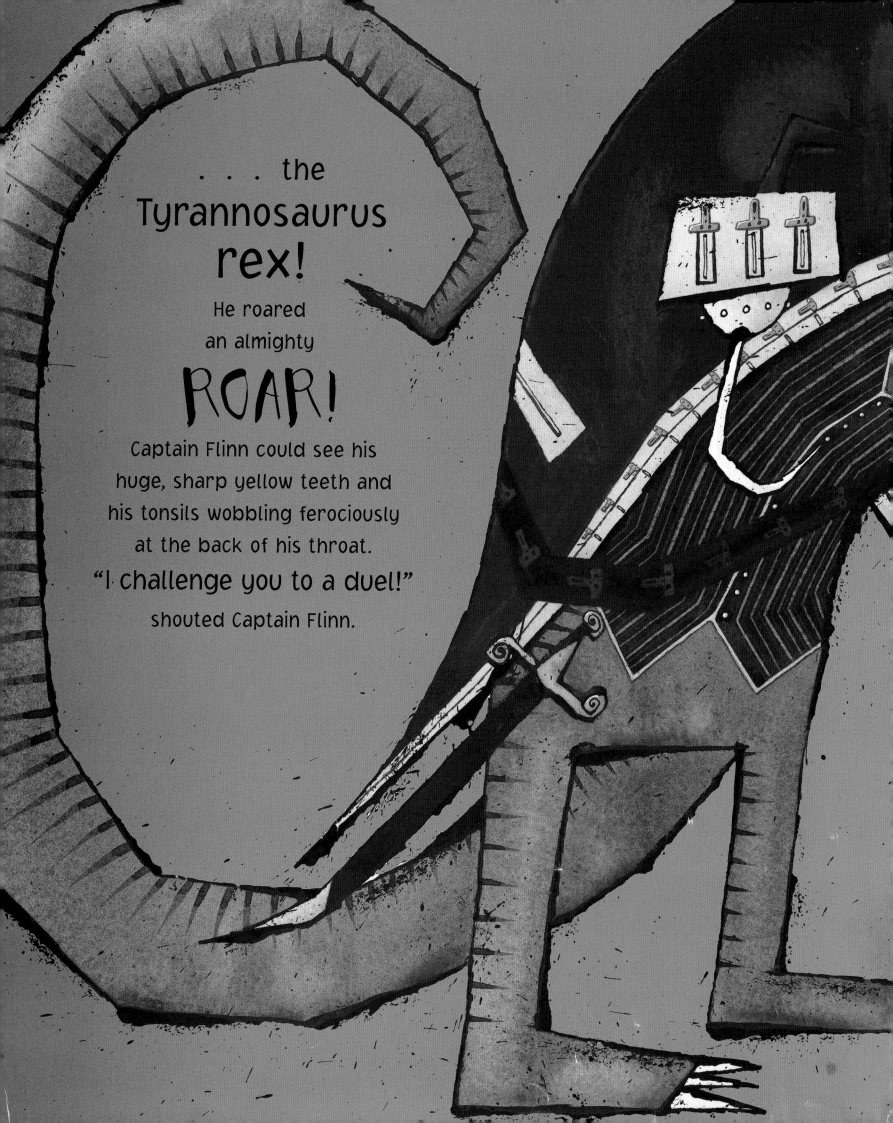

. . . the **Tyrannosaurus rex!**

He roared
an almighty

ROAR!

Captain Flinn could see his
huge, sharp yellow teeth and
his tonsils wobbling ferociously
at the back of his throat.

"I challenge you to a duel!"

shouted Captain Flinn.

"I'm going to cut you up
into little pirate sausages!"
yelled the Tyrannosaurus rex,
dribbling greedily. "Then I'm going
to put you on the barbecue and

EAT YOU UP!

With much too much ketchup!" he added.

"Oh no, you're not!" yelled Captain Flinn, and charged.
Their swords FLASHED and CRASHED and BASHED and SMASHED

for at least two hours and
twenty-five minutes until,
finally,

the Tyrannosaurus rex
was exhausted.

"Captain Flinn," he stammered, "I surrender.
You are such a great pirate that YOU should
be the captain of all the pirate dinosaurs!
Please spare me, and I promise I'll be the
best pirate in the world. Honest!"

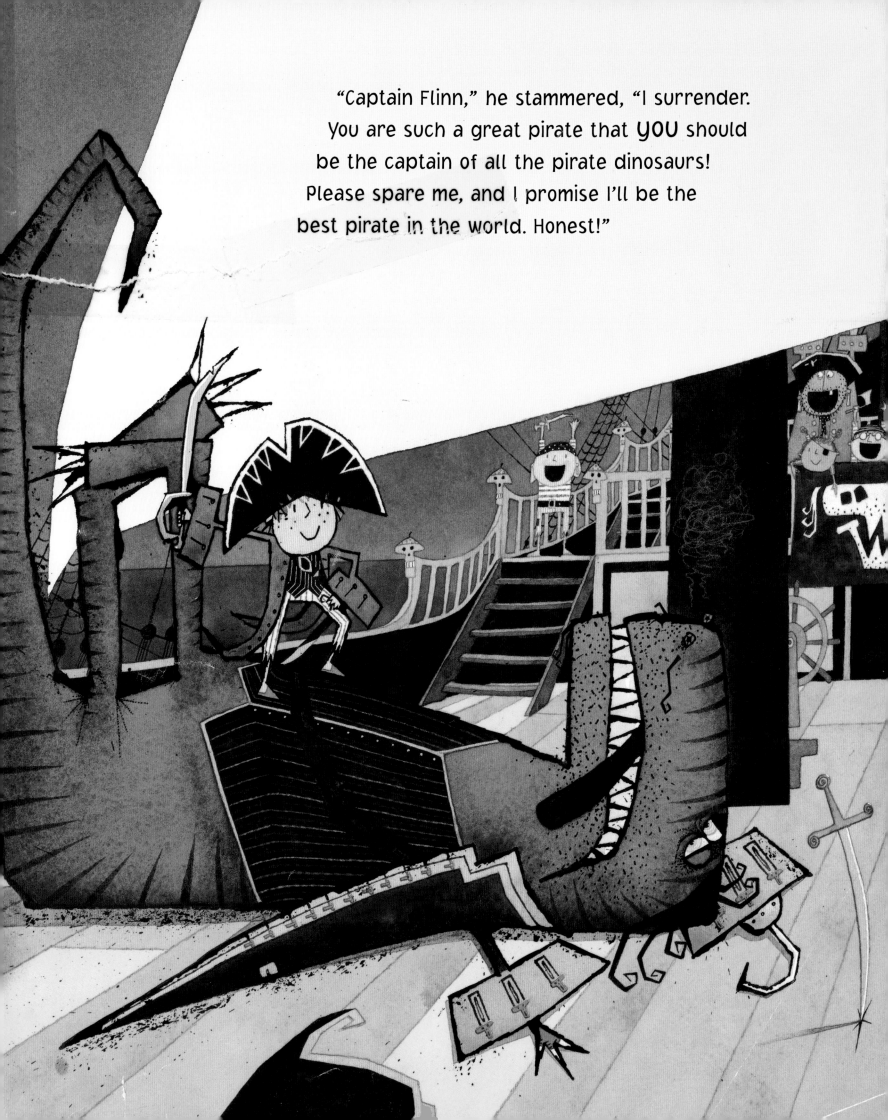

"Then maybe one day I will be your captain," replied Captain Flinn, "but now we'd better get back to school. It's almost lunchtime!"

So Captain Flinn took the wheel of the *Acorn*.
And while Pirate Pearl, Pirate Tom, and Pirate Violet
untied the crew, Stubble made a delicious fish stew.

When they got to the harbor, they waved good-bye to Captain Stubble and to the Tyrannosaurus rex.

Flinn saw that the door they had fallen through was still hanging open. So they all clambered in . . .

. . . and instantly they were back among
the paints and rolls of paper and pots of glue.
Flinn grabbed some markers, and they all crept
back into the classroom.

"And they all lived happily ever after," said Miss Pie, closing the book she had been reading. "You've been in that closet a long time, Flinn. What *have* you been doing?"

Flinn smiled secretly at his friends.

"Oh, nothing," he said.
"Nothing really at all."